BOY ON THE STEP

In the Outer Dark

Giraffe

How the Plains Indians Got Horses

Out-of-the-Body Travel

Summer Celestial

BOY
on the
STEP

poems by
STANLEY
PLUMLY

the ecco press
new york

The Ecco Press
26 West 17th Street, New York, N.Y. 10011
Published simultaneously in Canada by Penguin Books Canada Ltd., Ontario
Printed in the United States of America
Designed by Beth Tondreau Design/Jane Treuhaft
FIRST PAPERBACK EDITION

Thanks are due the editors of the following publications in which many of
these poems — some in altered versions — first appeared:
Antæus — "Above Barnesville," "Boy on the Step"; *The Atlantic Monthly* —
"Analogies of the Leaf," "Hedgerows"; *Crazyhorse* — "With Stephen in Maine";
Field — "Cloud Building," "Infidelity"; *The Indiana Review* — "Two Autumns"
(earlier versions of parts 4 and 10 of "Boy on the Step"); *The New Yorker* —
"Cedar Waxwing on Scarlet Firethorn," "Coming into La Guardia Late at
Night," "Early and Late in the Month," "Fountain Park," "Four Appaloosas,"
"The Wyoming Poetry Circuit"; *The Ohio Review* — "Birthday," "The Foundry
Garden," "Men Working on Wings"; *The Paris Review* — "Against Starlings";
Partisan Review — "The James Wright Annual Festival"; *Poets Respond to AIDS*
(Crown books) — "Pityriasis Rosea."
    Appreciation also to the Ingram-Merrill Foundation, the University of
Maryland, and the National Endowment for the Arts for grants that helped in
the completion of this book.
    The line "There's a river of birds in migration" ("The Six Shapes in Nature")
is from an anonymous medieval lyric.
    The epigraph is from Habakkuk 2:19.

LIBRARY OF CONGRESS CATALOGING-IN-PUBLICATION DATA

Plumly, Stanley.
    Boy on the step: poems / by Stanley Plumly.
        p. cm.: $9.95
    I. Title.
    [PS3566.L78B6 1991]   811'.54—dc20   91-15733 CIP

    ISBN 0-88001-229-3

The text of this book is set in Janson.

for William Matthews

CONTENTS

III

Woe unto him that saith to the wood, Awake

I

HEDGEROWS

How many names. Some trouble
or other would take me outside
up the town's soft hill, into the country,
on the road between them.
The haw, the interlocking bramble, the thorn,
head-high, higher, a corridor, black windows.
And everywhere the smell of sanicle
and tansy, the taste
of the judas elder, and somewhere
the weaver thrush that here they call mistle,
as in evergreen, because of the berries.
I'd walk in the evening,
into the sun, the blue air almost cold,
wind like traffic, the paper flowering of the ox-eye
and the campion still white,
still lit, like spring.
I'd walk until my mind cleared,
with the clarity of morning, the dew transparent
to the green, even here, in another
country, in the dark,
the hedgework building and weaving
and building under both great wings of the night.
I'd have walked to the top of the next
hill, and the next, the stars,
like town lights, coming on,
the next town either Ash Mill or Rose Ash.
Then sometimes a car, sometimes a bird, a magpie,
gliding. This is voicelessness,
the still breath easing.
I think, for a moment, I wanted to die,
and that somehow the tangle
and bramble, the branch and flowering of the hedge

would take me in, torn, rendered down
to the apple or the red wound or the balm,
   the green man, leaf and shred.
      I think I wanted the richness, the thickness,
   the whole dumb life gone to seed,
and the work to follow, the hedger with his tools,
   ethering and cutting, wood and mind.
      And later, in this life,
   to come back as a pail made of elm
or broom straw of broom or the heartwood of the yew
   for the bow, oak for the plow—
      the bowl on the wild cherry of the table for the boy
   who sits there, having come from the field
with his family, half hungry, half cold,
      one more day of the harvest accounted,
         yellowing, winnowing,
      the boy lost in the thought
of the turning of the year and the dead father.

ANALOGIES OF THE LEAF

Almost dark, late spring. And nothing in the chances
of the visible, first stars but a hunter and a ram
and women so virginal they give off fire
to light the pathway up the ladder to the stair—
nothing in the columnar night wind
but the hollowing of air,
the whistle empty at the tag end of the song.
Along the back, along the rainbow
vertebra, at the spear-point of the spine,
my hand cuts like a leaf. You turn and open,
as my mouth opens over yours.
When I enter you your face takes on
the focus of a thought suddenly
appropriate to how your knees have worked
up under my arms, your eyes shutting on the sources.
Then the blurred, spilled shape of the willow
finding water, letting its low branching down.

When the wind blows back against the leaves
they turn a kind of silver, like fish,
we said as kids, and rubbed them raw to watch
the flash and glitter come off clean in our soiled hands.
It never did, though we said it did.
And the rain that can turn leaves silver, quick as mercury—
something else for the hands to fail to catch.
The evening is scaled and set, counting blue
and blue and blue, the way a petal
or a stone is stained. You come down flushed,
then white and cool. The story of the body
is endless interiority,
following or not following the blood

back to the glassy breath—sympathetic
pathways, arterial, vaginal, thecal—
the spirit passed between us, mouth on mouth,
the soul so rooted in the other it is flesh.

AGAINST STARLINGS

1

Their song is almost painful the way it
penetrates the air—above the haze and
level of the fields a thin line drawn. A
wire. Where the birdcall goes to ground. But I'd
stand anyway under the oaks lining
the road and whistle, tireless with chances,
tossing, by the handful, the crushed stone.
All of them answered, none of them came down.
By evening there'd be hundreds filling the
trees past hearing, black along the branches.
They'd go off with the guns like buckshot, black,
filling the sky, falling. I held my ears.
The holes in the air closed quickly, then healed.
Birds were bloodless, like smoke, wind in a field—

2

But not to be confused with the cowbird,
its brown head, its conical sparrow's bill,
nor with the redwing, which is obvious,
even showy, blood or birthmark, nor with
the boat-tailed grackle—though at dusk, when they
gathered from the north, they were all blackbirds.
They were what the night brought, and the blown leaves,
and the cloud come down in the rain. The ease
of it, the way summer would be ending.
When I found one one morning it was the
color of oil in a pool of water,
bronze, blue-green, still shining. The parts that were
missing were throwaway, breast and belly
and the small ink and eye-ring of the eye—

3

Not to be compared with the last native
wild pigeon, trap-shot high in Pike County,
Ohio, the fourth day of spring, nineteen
hundred—thirty years after the harvest
of millions filled the buffalo trains east.
They were, by report, "the most numerous
bird ever to exist on earth," what the
Narragansett called Wuskowhan, the blue
dove, the wanderer, whose flight is silent.
Not to be compared with the smaller, wild
mourning dove, which haunted the afternoon,
which you heard all day till dark. They
were the sound in my sleep those long naps home,
the last train calling down the line in time—

4

Sometimes, at the far end of a pasture,
the burdock and buckwheat thick as the grass
along the hedgework, you could still find nests,
some fallen, some you had to climb to. They
were a kind of evidence, a kind of
science, sticks, straw, and brilliant bits of glass.
My mother had a hat like that, feathered,
flawed—she'd bought it used. It was intricate
and jeweled, the feathers scuffed like a jay's,
and so stiff you could've carried water.
The millinery species is over.
Those nests had nothing in them. Still, sometimes
I'd wait until the autumn light was gone,
the sky half eggshell, half a starling's wing—

5

Not to be compared with the fluted voice,
the five phrases in different pitches
of the thrush, the one Whitman heard, and Keats.
Sturnus vulgaris vulgaris—not to
be confused with the soft talk and music,
the voice that calls the spirit from the wood.
Those that stayed the winter sat the chimney
to keep warm, and cried down the snow to fly
against the cold. They were impossible.
They'd be dead before spring, or disappear
into the white air. —Not to be confused
with the black leaves whirling up the windward
side of the house, caught in the chimney smoke,
the higher the more invisible—

6

                    Black.
I saw them cover the sky over a
building once, and storm an alley. They were
a gathering, whole. Yet on the window-
sill, individual, stealing the grain
I put there, they'd almost look at me through
the glass. Something magical, practical.
They'd even graze the ground for what had dropped.
I wished for one to come into the house,
and left the window open just enough.
None ever did. That was another year.
What is to be feared is emptiness and
nothing to fill it. I threw a stone or
I didn't throw a stone is one language—
the vowel is a small leaf on the tongue.

CEDAR WAXWING ON
SCARLET FIRETHORN

To start again with something beautiful,
and natural, the waxwing first on one
foot, then the other, holding the berry
against the moment like a drop of blood—
red-wing-tipped, yellow at the tip of the
tail, the head sleek, crested, fin or arrow,
turning now, swallowing. Or any bird
that turns, as by instruction, its small, dark
head, disinterested, toward the future; flies
into the massive tangle of the trees, slick.
The visual glide of the detail blurs.

The good gun flowering in the mouth is done,
like swallowing the sword or eating fire,
the carnival trick we could take back if
we wanted. When I was told suicide
meant the soul stayed with the body locked in
the ground I knew it was wrong, that each bird
could be anyone in the afterlife,
alive, on wing. Like this one, which lets its
thin lisp of a song go out into
the future, then follows, into the wood-
land understory, into its voice, gone.

But to look down the long shaft of the air,
the whole healing silence of the air, fire
and thorn, where we want to be, on the edge
of the advantage, the abrupt green edge
between the flowering pyracantha and
the winded, open field, before the trees—
to be alive in secret, this is what
we wanted, and here, as when we die what
lives is fluted on the air—a whistle,
then the wing—even our desire to die,
to swallow fire, disappear, be nothing.

The body fills with light, and in the mind
the white oak of the table, the ladder
stiffness of the chair, the dried-out paper
on the wall fly back into the vein and
branching of the leaf—flare like the waxwings,
whose moment seems to fill the scarlet hedge.
From the window, at a distance, just more
trees against the sky, and in the distance
after that everything is possible.
We are in a room with all the loved ones,
who, when they answer, have the power of song.

for John Jones

THE WYOMING POETRY CIRCUIT

Climbing down out of the rain, which is what
the breakable upper branches were: rain:
webbed, hardly visible vessels, the imprint
of the leaves long since Cambrian, Ordovician,
rooted out of time, the cold breakable
rain branching out of sight, but thicker
the lower down you went, thickest at the trunk . . .

My father had put me up there to look
for deer, above the scent. I never got
it right—it all looked rain to me,
the star-points at a distance blurring
with the trees. Two other moments: one
with friends in a great field in the spring,
the cold sky filled or emptied out of wind,

the Steller's jays angry or friendly depending,
then suddenly a redwing flies into
my hand just long enough to take the bread.
I can see the spots, like a starling's,
and the clipped, blood reds lit within the wing—
it is amazing, a moment, and nothing.
And the other: above the Wind River

Basin, in moon country, along the skyline,
the loose trail of antelope drifting
with the herds—heraldic, half wild, following
the traffic down to better pasture,
dead meat and following to slaughter.
We have to stop the truck to let them pass:
they congregate in front of us, like cages.

Light then dusk passes through them. Wyoming
is dusk, all day—I remember it seemed
deeper in the air, layers of the inter-
tonguing rock permeable, passable, like rain,
like a storm in daylight passing to the north,
the Indian towns starving with the dark,
the ranches poor with oil or coal or the

animal debt of the land, which had a shine
like dry seabeds or maria, silver,
though they held their shadow. In Sheridan
we met in a hunting lodge to talk,
no one from anywhere you could name,
who loved the place or got stuck—we talked into
the night, the still walls lined with signs and wonders.

Love will never let us alone, which is
exactly what it does. That night it got
too late. Even outside, in moonlight,
we could see our faces, people you'd never
see again, who'd traveled hundreds of miles
in a landscape through stone just to talk
or hear the poem read against silence.

The next morning was winter, the rain
ice cold, October, but by afternoon
clear with the smell of snow. All those towns to
get through, all that endless gradual ground.
At Wind River the walls were stratified,
like ladder variations on the color
stone, a ladder to be dreamed of climbing

from the earth—we stopped to watch the river move
its tons of trainloads of the rock. My friend
said that stone is what they have instead of
trees, which are immortal, flowering out of
stone like souls in secret. I could believe
it, counting the outcrop few leading toward
the horizon. The small stone in the hand,

she said, is for loneliness, company,
good luck. To the south, past Rawlins, there were
elk, like shale and mud and blue dusk, part of a cut
that had climbed out of the river: animals
part tree, part stone, coming down, she said,
to feed with the herds, to take a look at us,
but not too close, or close, or not at all.

for Gretel Ehrlich

TOWARD UMBRIA

It isn't the poppies,
their red and accidental numbers,
nor the birdfoot-violets, their blue lines
wasted, nor the sheer, uninterrupted
wayside pastures—nor along the river
the centuries-faded terra-cotta farmhouses,
outbuildings, floatings of iron, iron windmills,
                                        pastoral or neutral,
like the ancient towns walled-up in sunlight
and the failed machinery left abandoned.
From a summer I can still see the sidewalk
broken by a root and follow, in a thought,
the bull-blue thistle wild along the fence-wire
into the country. Here the thistle blooms

too tall, the color of clover, Great Marsh and Musk,
and spiked like roses. Something about its
conference and size, its spine indifference—.
                        We are drift and flotsam,
though sometimes when we stop to look out over
the landscape, outcrops of limestone and a few
stone sheep, the ground itself seems torn,
and when we drive along the white glide of the river,
the high wheat grass like water in the wind,
someone in joy running from the house,
the story is already breaking down.
The season is ending, fire on the wing,
or the season is starting endlessly again,
sedge and woodrush and yellow chamomile,

anywhere a field is like a wall, lapsed, fallow
or filled, a stain of wildflowers or a wave
of light washing over stone, everything in time,
                                    and all the same—
if I pick this poppy, as I used to
pull up weeds, wild strawberries, anything,
a city will be built, we'll have to live there,
we'll have to leave. Once, and in one direction only.
And the figure on the landscape coming toward us
will be someone we knew and almost loved, or loved,
for whom this moment is equally awkward,
as for those ahead of us it is equally condemned,
ploughmen and gleaners, shepherds-of-the-keep,
                        those on the road, those lost.

BIRTHDAY

An old mortality, these evening doorways into rooms,
this door from the kitchen and there's the yard,
the grass not cut and filled with sweetness,
and in the thorn the summer wounding of the sun.

And locked in the shade the dove calling down.

The glare's a little blinding still but only
for the moment of surprise, like suddenly
coming into a hall with a window at the end,

the light stacked up like scaffolding. I am
that boy again my father told not to look
at the ground so much looking at the ground.

I am the animal touched on the forehead, charmed.

In the sky the silver maple like rain in a cloud
we've tied: and I see myself walking from what looks like
a classroom, the floor waxed white, into my father's
arms, who lifts me, like a discovery, out of this life.

II

CLOUD BUILDING

All night there'd have been
an anger in the air, terror of voices, threats,
   the argument half dreamt, then calm,
         then the hard doors shutting
   into sleep and cold and waking with the sun.
I'd have risen for school and made a hole
      in the window ice to see through:
         blown piles of the inches
      of snow, and in between, like ponds,
the blue-brittle surfaces with a high blue
   cirrus shine, exactitude of color
         in the eye. Even the brightness
   and shape of the smoke coming
from the chimney were divinations of the wind,
      the body broadcast, the winter leaf let go.
      Say a bird had hit the glass,
      first light, like a snowball with a stone,
tossed at remarkable distance.
   At the cool heights of the mind
         it should have been a cardinal
   or a jay, something with color,
something to see instead of a piece of something,
      nothing but gray ice stony broken.
         And now it comes in a dish,
      in the new year, melted, white
as albumen, as water in a bowl, or else so dry
   you could blow it back to crystal.
         It comes back now in the least
   disguise as paper and ash,
the day's first fire falling back on the house
      in a story with the wind, a ragtag
         starling, or crying, the snowy

light crazy with perfection.
You hold a thing just dead it will burn
  in your hand like a lie told to the body.
    You hold someone in your arms,
    the cloud of sperm still drifting like a spirit,
you think she'll disappear, the heart
    immaculate. The cold radiance—
      it wants a white light dry as dust
      in the eye; it wants to leave
the body through the mouth and come back slowly,
  pure with patience, shine slowly
    as something else we'll never know
  except alone, like the sentimental
old, who are full of stories,
    or children, who in solitude have silence.

INFIDELITY

The two-toned Olds swinging sideways out of
the drive, the bone-white gravel kicked up in
a shot, my mother in the deathseat half
out the door, the door half shut—she's being
pushed or wants to jump, I don't remember.
The Olds is two kinds of green, hand-painted,
and blows black smoke like a coal-oil fire. I'm
stunned and feel a wind, like a machine, pass
through me, through my heart and mouth; I'm standing
in a field not fifty feet away, the
wheel of the wind closing the distance.
Then suddenly the car stops and my mother
falls with nothing, nothing to break the fall . . .

One of those moments we give too much to,
like the moment of acknowledgment of
betrayal, when the one who's faithless has
nothing more to say and the silence is
terrifying since you must choose between
one or the other emptiness. I know
my mother's face was covered black with blood
and that when she rose she too said nothing.
Language is a darkness pulled out of us.
But I screamed that day she was almost killed,
whether I wept or ran or threw a stone,
or stood stone-still, choosing at last between
parents, one of whom was driving away.

ABOVE BARNESVILLE

In the body the night sky in ascension—
the starry campion, the mallow rose, the wild potato vine.
You could pick them, though they'd die in your hand.
It's here, in the thirties, that the fathers panned for gold,
pick-and-shovel, five-to-a-dollar-a-day—you could survive
panning the glacial drift, the split rock, the old alluvial scar.
If you climb the brickpath back to the top of the hill,
for the long hard look, you can still see Quaker poverty,
the sheer tilt of the green-gray roll of the land,
the rock-soil thinning out, the coal breaking ground like ice.
Some of the farmers still use horses for fear of the height, the
        weight against them,
as all the working day you can walk to the abrupt edge
of property and watch machines opening the earth.
The valley, the locals call it,
a landscape so deadly the water pools to oil before it clears—
a kind of kerosene, a few dropped stars or sunlight.

Deep autumnal nights I imagine my parents lying side
by side on the good grass looking up at the coal-and-diamond
        dark,
as they will lie together for the rest of their lives.
The star lanes scatter, and disappear. I will be born
under the sign of the twins less than a mile from here,
with too much blood on the floor. My father, right now,
is turning toward my mother. In the doctrine of signatures
the body is divisible, the heart the leaf of a redbud
or the blue ash in a fire, the genitalia
the various and soft centers of the shell
or the long spathe and cleft, the pink pouch of the flower.
They will be waking soon.

Overhead the chill and endless pastoral of the sky, the
    constellations drifting.
For a moment the mirror is laid beside us—Cassiopeia, Ursa
Minor, the Plow—parts of the house, a door left open, a
    window,
so that we can see how far down into the earth the path is
    leading.

The word for wood is xylem, which is the living tissue,
and by a kind of poetry graduates inward
from summer to winter to sapwood to the heart.
I was with my father the day he found
the tree that had been gouged and rendered useless and cut
    down.
It was probably hickory or walnut, black, the dull bark split
and furrowed, like a field: it seemed a hundred feet,
most of it in branches, the feathering of leaves turning color at
    the top.
The size of it, so suddenly alone.
My father, in his anger, cut away until the wood was soft . . .
In the rain the smell of tannin, fire and char, poignant on the
    air.
I remember how thin the upper branches were, intricate as
    nests,
how impossible to climb this high without falling, breaking
    through.
It seemed to have come down from the sky in stages—
the broken branches first, then the medulla and the root,
then, deep inside, the lumber flying at the brain.

At night, sometimes, you could hear the second shift,
and fantasize the train's elliptical passage through the town
or the mythical ocean pulling moonlight from your windows.
You could hear the celestial traffic taking off.
But in the morning, crack-white and plain, it would be nothing
but the earth made new again, a little less each time.
Once, one of those pure October days that seem to rise,
I came up over the scab-hill of a mine—all slag and oxidation,
the sick ground running orange in a stream, here and there
the skeletons of buildings. It looked like parts of a great
        abandoned house
ruined in a fire in the middle of a woods saved by snow.
It had seasons, memory—
nothing like the Dipper-sized machines
digging into the hillsides by the houseful.
A month ago I could have picked wildflowers, corn-blues and
        goldenrod,
while in the summer I'd have never found the place in so much
        green.

In the constellation named for the bottles tossed to the side of
        the road,
for the poverty of leaves blowing one-way down the lane,
for the stones flecked like fish, for the water carried with both
        hands closed,
the stars are of the sixth and seventh magnitude.
You can hardly see them in the broken glass and the ash from
        the burn-off.
In the coal-colored dark it's all pinholes and candles,
and this is as close as we'll ever get,

as when we close our eyes something gossamer like nebula
    floats up.
I told my father not to die, but he didn't listen.
He got down on his knees as if to hold on to the earth,
as if to hide inside his body.
In the black and crystalline light of coal and rock,
through the flake and mica leaves, layer upon layer,
he would not climb the ladder so loved by believers.
For that I love him, and find him safe
in the least of things alive—dust on the road, wind at its back.

Those first cold nights you could taste the ice in the air.
North seemed to mean the stars, where the snow came from.
Even now you could see it start to fall. Sides of the trees white
with it, heelprints and tire-tracks white with it,
the little edges of the roofs, like the drawing in the kitchen,
    white with it.
If we could make it cold enough and snow enough, such
    silence!
Even now, with color in the leaves, you could almost see it
    falling.
My mother called it the ocean, the way it covered everything,
the way in the morning the light of it was blinding.
She'd watch it for hours, letting it fall.
I think of her following my father as if by a miracle of leverage,
the one pulling the other out to sea. I think of how I will
    follow her,
how she brought me here, half her body, half of the rest of her.
Those nights the constellation shapes glistened into water
I thought it was forever, I thought it was enough,
though I knew that if water rises stones will burn.

PITYRIASIS ROSEA

We say the blood rose, meaning it came to the surface
like a bruise, which comes from outside, blue, in a small
        violence,
a stone, a brush against the table, the punishment of riches;
or meaning the deep object, the blood rose, which is artifice,
since in nature what to look for is color neutral, mallow,
a little pale, like florals years on the canvas, themselves
a kind of nature now with the light and dust in the room's
atmosphere; or meaning the viral air picked out this blood
to rise like the rash after sex, which darkly pollinates
the skin, delicate, in a rush of the blood returning, like
a weight of ash, to the heart, except that here it comes
in petal-, sepal-sized extrusions, but softer, like embarrassment,
the flaw a fire-leak in the blood, hectic, risen, flush
on the upper body with passion, intermission, mouth of
        the kiss.

The sickle, the scythe in the blood, which means to sweep
the tide of its impurities, like a sword in the wave, cuts, fails,
rises like a thorn—we say this too is the blood burning clean.
But only the wren flower, yarrow, or the nettle will heal the old
wound or the dry bleeding, which made the flesh blush even
        to itself
and the boy on the hillside, working in a fever of the summer
against the wire of undergrowth, walk away, because his hands
wouldn't close. The raw rose on the back of my hand is a sign
of the season, something in the air, like pollen and the garden

phlox we let grow wild, sick purple, pink, what a child or a
     man
might worry meant corruption of the purest part, the blood,
which is immortal and fire on the river running backward,
     forward
in a wind, dangerous, anonymous as any other part of ourselves
passed on, scattered, or poured back into the earth.

THE FOUNDRY GARDEN

Myths of the landscape—
the sun going down in the mouths of the furnaces,
the fires banked and cooling, ticking into dark, here and there
    the sudden flaring into roses,
then the light across the long factory of the field, the split and
    rusted castings,
across the low slant tin-roofs of the buildings, across fallow and
    tar and burnt potato ground . . .
Everything a little still on fire, in sunlight, then smoke, then
    cinder,
then the milling back to earth, rich earth, the silica of ash.
The times I can taste the iron in the air, the gray wash like
    exhaust, smell the burn-off,
my eyes begin to tear, and I'm leaning against a wall, short of
    breath,
my heart as large as my father's, alone in such poverty my
    body scars the light.
Arable fields, waste and stony places, waysides—
the day he got the job at the Wellbaum and Company Foundry
    he wept,
and later, in the truck, pulled the plug on a bottle.
In the metallurgy of ore and coal and limestone, in the
    conversion of the green world to gray,
in the face of the blue-white fire, I remember the fencerow, the
    white campion,
calyx and coronal scales, and the hawthorns, cut to the size of
    hedge,
the haws so deep in the blood of the season they bled.
The year we were poor enough to dig potatoes we had to drive
    there,
then wait for the men to leave who let the fires go out.

There'd be one good hour of daylight, the rough straight rows
    running into shade.
We'd work the ground until the sun was a single line.
I can see my father now cut in half by the horizon, coming
    toward me, both arms weighted down.
I can see him bending over, gone.
Later, in the summer, I'd have painted the dead rust undulant
    sides of all the buildings aluminum,
which in the morning threw a glare like water on the garden.

MEN WORKING ON WINGS

In dreams they were everything hurt
whose faces were always coming into focus
like a feeling never before realized
offered now as longing,

but not spiritual, like the cloud
in marble or the flaws in sunlight
streaking through the window,
but palpable, the way

that cloud, those flaws take on
the human. If I have to choose I choose
those nights I sat in the dark
in the Mote Park outfield

waiting with my father for the long
flyballs that fell more rarely than the stars.
We'd talk or he'd hit the hole
in his glove. A hundred

times he'd hit the hole in his glove.
In his factory wool-and-cotton gray
uniform he looked like a soldier
too young to fight,

like his sailor brother
and our monkey uncle doughboy Harry who'd
been gassed in the trenches—
too young to fight.

But nobody died. Once, on the Ponte
S. Angelo, leading from the Castle of Angels
     across a wrist of the Tiber,
          I watched the artisans

          of the working classes work with the patience
of repairmen on the backs of the immortelles.
     Except for their hands they sat
          the wings in stillness,

          hammer and chisel, like any other sculptors—
the job endless, infinitesimal, a constancy
     of detail, the air itself
          the enemy,

          and the long gold light pouring down.
The big, flat, dead leaves of the sycamores
     would whirl around them in a theme,
          then drift like paper

          to the river. The leaves might float,
in another life, all the way to the sea,
     spotted and brown like the backs
          of the hands of the old.

     The wings of the angels were stone clouds
stained, pocked like a bird's. My father
     didn't want to die, nor my uncles,
          in their fifties,

nor dull Jack Bruning, who'd have welded
wings to his back to get another day of drinking,
and who claimed that in the war
he'd eaten a man's flesh.

At each other's funerals they were
inconsolable—they would draw from the scabbard,
with its lime-green rust, a sword
against this death,

they would not be turned away.
In their flawed hearts they would stand fast,
side by side, as in a photograph,
youngest to tallest,

as on the bridge, with half-closed eyes
and mouths about to speak, the twelve
Bernini angels, in their cold
and heavy robes,

and wings unfurled with the weight of men,
were in alignment yet reluctant to pass
from this to the next sleep.
And who would know—

and what would they tell us?

THE SIX SHAPES IN NATURE

There's a river of birds in migration
too late into the season to be real.
Like a thought turned in a machination

it seems more likely in imagination,
though there it is in fact with what we feel.
There's a river of birds in migration.

The loss I felt of pure concentration—
I thought my heart was broken. That was real,
not just a thought in a machination.

The height and arc of the birds, formation
on formation—and then to watch them reel
like a river turning in migration—

is nothing if not an inspiration
to let go, if not too late, of the feel
of the thing, its endless machination.

But to give the thought to the emotion,
not let the feeling soar—this too is real,
though the river of birds in migration
is too far in the year's machination.

FOUNTAIN PARK

At a hundred feet or more the maples
and the oaks are another architecture
building on this life the gold leaf of the next,
scattered in sequence, linked like windbreak.
No matter how miraculous the stiff
flight of the fish or the balance of gifted
children on their toes, no matter that the god
has drawn his sword against his nakedness
and the lily is a girl closed against the cold,
I can't remember when the fountains worked,
spread like all the other cemetery
sculpture into a city in a valley,
here and there the graveyard grass like pasture.

From the top of the hill it's Saturday,
empty, early in the evening, in season,
the sun in detail now, a kind of tone,
a kind of candlepower the wind could easily
blow out, the way it kindles the dry leaves
in the bowls of the fountains—pillars of
fire, water from a stone. In the bridgework
of the leaves I'm holding, the nine-lobed oak,
the compound willow feather, all kinds of things
pass witness and are true about this last
light of the day coming onto winter,
the trees almost transparent in their dark,
the high grass green as lawns in the hereafter.

WITH STEPHEN IN MAINE

The huge mammalian rocks in front of the lawn,
domestic between the grass and the low tide—
Stephen has set his boat in one of the pools,
his hand the little god that makes it move.
It is cold, the sky the rough wool and gabardine
of pictures someone almost talented has painted.
Off and on the sun, then Stephen is wading . . .

Yesterday we saw two gulls shot out of the sky.
One of them drifted into shore, broken, half eaten,
green with the sea. When I found it this morning
all I could think to do was throw it back. One wing.
Its thin blood spread enough that Stephen is finger-
printed and painted with washing and wiping dry.
Even his boat, at the watermark, is stained.

I lift him, put him up on top of my shoulders.
From here he can watch the deep water pile, turn over.
He says, with wonder, that it looks like the ocean
killing itself. He wants to throw stones, he wants
to see how far his boat can sail, will float.
The mile or more from here to there is an order of color,
pitched white and black and dove- or green-gray, blue,

but far and hurt from where he is seeing.

III

VICTORY HEIGHTS

Five, six, seven stories high: you could throw
    a ball to the roof, lose it in the air,
in the dusk that picks apart white objects.
    Someone so old her face is wild is looking
out the window from the ground floor, the small,
    knit, candle-colored lights of the building
linking into code. No one to forgive
    the animal its eyes. Start anywhere,
start here, with the street noise like a kind of
    snow, with your head underwater, held in
place by the dumbbell too big for his clothes,
    his hands like a farmer's holding a calf
hard by the ears, the water the dull, ditch
    caramel of flooding right after rain:
we sort of swim there, stripped, the three feet
    of water rushing ungated between
conduits, warm, thicker than water: and
    he is holding my head down because he
has the reddest hair and the whitest skin,
    and lets go only after the urine
has passed over me. At the corner
    it is spring, the early twilight water
blue, the scarves of the high clouds dissolving:
    the streetlight's on and down off the hill
the lights in the houses painted every
    other year come on, like the sky turned over.
You look up into the artificial
    glare, the insects and the electric hum
only just now gathering to gain
    momentum. The night will go blind white
or you will close your eyes: all around you
    row after row of the civilian barracks

of the postwar, everybody's radio
too loud, wafting or following the scent.
The little rooms, the little chicken yards,
the dirty crosses for the clothesline rope,
blood of the lamb wiped on the garden walls:
in school the story is the Passover,
the sign to save the child: and I know the way
I know fear that I need saving, and that
the blood is real, somebody's, something's care,
and that under the street at the blackpools,
in the soft, wet sections of the fields,
in the brickwalk, in the long serial
counting of the bricks, the flat black of the
trapdoor opens: and it is not death but
the body-to-be and the invalid
soul forming or floating on the waters.

FOUR APPALOOSAS

First the glycerin, green transparency of rain,
the stations of the air shifting around them, in columns,
like the trees, next to which they stand in a kind
of pattern, even the one at the fence watching the traffic,
all of them stained like stone, mud and gray and pearl,
backs to the wind. Then the gulls coming down,
like lights, out of a cloud . . . ice white.
The sea is yoked but huge against the ground, tidal
in its weather, only miles from here. You feel its weight
in the shapes of things, antipodal, bent-nail,
the scarring of the branches black and lateral,
the rain suddenly visible at angles mixed with snow.
Now the shorebirds are the knocked-off hats of the horses . . .
Now the snow sticking white to the windshield.

EARLY AND LATE IN THE MONTH

1   *Paddington Recreation Ground*

White birds on the cold green winter grass, wet
with white, like snow held too long in the hand,
the runner's white breath ghosting the gray air.
The morning is one thing, then another—
rain, sometimes the sun slick along the trees,
sometimes the sudden thought of clouds settling
for the day, then lifting. While I slept none
of this was here, none of this drifting, though

I remember in the evening I watched
the sky hurt with the blue at the cold quick
of all color, then grow dark, and darker,
infinitely. The day moon held the moon.
I watched sunlight, hard against the windows,
disappear, watched the brickwork leave the dull-
red row of buildings, watched the street turn black
and electric, and finally oil with ice.

I woke up cold, like a boy late for school,
the photographic air granular, alive,
then lay almost an hour sorting nothing
from nothing, waiting for the room to fill.
Outside, in the half-rain, half-snow, half snow
themselves, the birds had gathered from the tide.
The man on the track was running away,
dressed in the cold colors of the morning.

All afternoon the industrial light
of London dissolving into rain, the
sexual, interminable patchwork
of the plane trees piling in perspective.
Silver and copper, like money in the
street, brilliant through the large upper window.
My eye, hooked like a bird's, fixes on any-
thing, even in memory: how the black rain
washes clean, how the dry leaf opens and
is lifted whole back into the new wind.
The spirit puts its nose against the glass—
the sky is nothing, is a starved black wing.
Below: the mirror tops of cars, the warped
iron railing the kids will try to tightwalk.

THE JAMES WRIGHT
ANNUAL FESTIVAL

That night we flew into Pittsburgh where Tom Flynn met the plane to drive us back to Ohio just over the river into Belmont County where we were to meet Galway and the hosts of the Second Annual James Wright Festival for supper and the chatter of a late night before the first day of readings. What I remember from the long ride in from the airport—a new spring night with constellations broken and the blurred edges of the foothills building against the wind in a wall up from the river—is the dark and how it came into the car at a speed we understood, how it filled in the small lights going out everywhere behind us, how it moved on our faces; how later, after dinner, all of us tiring, it touched all our faces. What I remember from Galway's face that night is how the next day he talked about the work, up until the end, on the last book, or didn't talk but got lost in the moment of the last poem of *that Vence morning many times since*, and how he waited there, in thought, with the many sources. On the Sunday I spent the empty early morning wandering too, lost in Martins Ferry, where down the street from the library the Heslop Brothers were still in business and farther still the WPA Swimming Pool Project plaque shone like a war memorial object. And I walked down to the water, the beautiful Ohio, Depression-wide all the way to Wheeling, and saw that whatever the working terrors are they are worse over there, on the other side, laid off, sabbath or dead-time on the line, where hell is still a foundry and a glassworks and an icehouse filled with coal, where they take you, out of pity, in the morning before daylight and bring you back in the evening, fire in the sun, white-of-the-eye-of-the-moon; and that even the petty farmers, our fathers, had come down from the farms to cross. James Wright, Galway would finally say, had gone to the end of the table, which we will earn, as we earn the daily bread set before us, and in Galway's face, in the room of the gathered that day, you could see the winter daybreak poem take form, in a whole other country, in high gold Mediterranean air but lifted here like stone or lumber flat above the river.

ARGUMENT & SONG

Like the piping of plenty, the mocker
and the starling, somebody calling from the stair,
the sister who went blind
in the head, then
mad, who loved the evening dark

like this one now, half dark, and loved
the glitter in the trees. You love the lawn,
the distance of the traffic,
the distant threats
of rain, though the air is in the way,

visible as rain, your blindness real,
and could we clear it the wing over the light
would disappear. You love
just sitting here,
one thing after another, the flowering

milk-white of the apple, my face a voice,
a color. I will never have a child.
You know this with an almost kindness
or anger, as if
to forgive a fact, as when the child

in the river rushes is let go,
sent ahead into the next life but never arrives
or arrives on the back of the
blood of a stone,
limestone, stela, ready for sacrifice;

as when the parents in the ghetto in Warsaw
in nineteen thirty-nine let the bleeders
    of the Beth Din visit on
      Fridays for kosher
samples of the blood. The boy in school

    who had my name and spoke poor English
and had a scar would point like a needle to the place
    on his arm where he was saved
      and told to live.
I think of him when I think of harm,

    the ambiguity of the birth-blood on the floor,
the fine-line healing of the mind, the bruise
    or the scar like a birthmark,
      and because I watched
you once after the third time they had opened

    you, watched you drift back and forth
under the white mask and the wounds. I thought
    you were dead, thought
      you were death,
and could see your ghost in the snow

    in the air above you. Coming awake
you wept, dreaming backward through the grief,
    the way a woman unloved for
      years is suddenly
entered, broken, left cold again,

and lies there certain she has conceived;
the way you lay awake with me those hours
the water would not break,
wept blindly
at the stillness of this child,

the choices like a ringing in the ears.
These shapes, these apple trees and maples, the blue
air hovering near rain, sounds
of the world,
nothing to be named but understood

among the phantoms and the callers—
that boy is dead who was afraid to bleed,
and all the fathers of
the bleeders;
there is no father, only fathering,

the whistle in the blood, the mother
on her back, the child-to-be at the doorway waiting.
When you used to tell me
I was lucky to be
alive, having left so much of myself

inside you, tipped and spilled and caught up
in the cord, I knew I would need a witness
and would fail, and that any
other loneliness
than this would be impossible.

COMING INTO LA GUARDIA
LATE AT NIGHT

The glide almost outside of time, the plane
at landing speed. It's January, dead
clear as starlight, the city in the air,
the Manichean pitch-black of the buildings
six thousand feet up the window mountain.
Adrift and north: Capella, Canis Minor.
In another year, leaving the city
in a car, I could see in the mirror
from the backbone of the bridge the wet sun
sliding into just one building, gold on
gold, and into the shadow wells. Like those
blossoms that fall to earth from light-years off,
some of the fire stays, some floats like torches
passed ahead of us along the pathways.

BOY ON THE STEP

1

He's out of breath only halfway up the hill,
which is brickwalk, awkward, and just steep enough
his mother's letting him rest but all the while
coaxing—there's like a climber's rope gone slack
between them, the thing you trip when your eye goes
from her face to his and then his arm, the left
one, off at the elbow, wrapped in heavy gauze.
This is none of your business yet intimate,
the way surprise is open, vulnerable,
the way the woman who came up to you was
anyone, pretty, so innocent of guile
you thought she was lost until she got too close
and the child in her turned hard, scared, her hand thrust
out for change, anything, wounds in the air, rest.

2

Gray forest earths. Across the street from the Church
of Pilgrims, Taras Shevchenko is alone
with his audience, who understand bondage
and the freedom of the street. He's a genius
of the independent life of the spirit
and speaks in poetry—they answer him in
lines that cut into the marble at his feet,
as those in love or angry mark a tree. The
broken glass and beer cans celebrate the space
of this island whose height is statuary,
stationary in the human. With distance
you can watch at night the match-fires, hear the sounds
of the small talk of exile, witness, transience,
articulate, American, close to ground.

3

Once, in a foreign city I knew, I was
lost, really lost. Nights running I slept outside—
days I'd walk astonished, ten miles, more, then circle.
The loneliness was like belief in something,
like carrying a nail tight inside the hand.
There was blood in my shoe, I could taste its salt
like sweetness in my mouth. And the windows were
tireless, and the worn maps of stone. One long night
outside Victoria Station I sat with
those for whom nothing's forsworn, all forsaken.
They tipped their bottles the way they held hands,
to keep out the cold and only to connect.
If they were lost they'd thought the heart of it through
enough to commiserate, curse loss, and piss.

4

A prophecy of mist—it came in October
in the morning up from the river and the
railyard, from smoke of the low fires banked inside
the yellow and the red trees, smoke like steam from
the work trains, stalled, waiting to be loaded, smoke
that rising early with the whistle you could
float out into, like sending forth the spirit.
I see those train lights now coming in, in fog,
or carlights passing with men going off to work,
the business of the night still left inside the
business of the day: that rain like silk still
holding. Things in such light are fragmentary,
cold, and reconnected later in forms we
might not recognize as friendly or history.

5

None of us dies entirely—some of us, all
of us sometimes come back sapling, seedling, cell,
like second growth, slowly, imperceptibly,
in the imprint of rings that wind like music
written down, in notes and bars, scale and silence.
Even the child, who was immortal, becomes
purity, anonymity inside us.
Which is why to watch a tree turn into fire
or fall is like a second death, like the grace
in stillness gone, exploded, fatal, final,
as someone loved, within whose face we confused
the infinite with the intimate, is last
a name, the point of a green leaf drawn across
the heart, whose loss is felt, though invisible.

6

The way the elms die is autumnal, yellow,
defoliate, long years in death, though the wound
is superficial since the heart- and sapwood
are already dead—you could find it with a
pocketknife, as if it were mold and natural.
These were wonderful, their famous fountain branch-
ing pendulous, both sides of the street, medieval,
tall as the cold ceilings in churches, endless
with extinction. Stephen, who is nine and would
need a ladder just to reach the least first branch,
can't believe they're gone, because he's heard of them
and sees them everywhere in other trees, as
if a tree could haunt a tree, like the Horace
Webster elm, which survives by luck of science.

7

Nineteen forty-five—whipsaws, handsaws, wedges
and hammers, half the men handicapped or old.
They seem old. Yet they take down the trees with care,
let them break and overlap on the whole street,
everything in sight domestic or half wild,
like countryside. It will be hours of cutting,
chain-pull and hauling before North Kent is cleared.
Later, with every other mother and child,
I'll look down into the deep well of an elm,
phloem and cambium, into the annual
rings and rays, into the pool where the leaf was
dropped, where the saws burned at angles where the rain
had poured, turned hard, into the waters of trees
where the blue stones and the white stones are a hill.

8

Woodsmoke rising among hundreds, thousands
of feet of trees, the thrashers signing, counter-
signing the morning—after breakfast the crews
can cut till noon without stopping. I'm amazed
at the level of the noise, the choral sawing,
the monkey-chatter of the men, the bridge-work
of branches falling. It hurts as much to hear
as see: then one of the men is falling, his
absolute voice abrupt against silence.
He's able to rise, and run, and knock me down—
he's holding out his hand, woodspikes through its palm.
He's on fire. I think I see flame on his arm.
When they catch him he's numb, already laved in
blood, blood as I've never seen, blood and sobbing.

9

To bring the hardwoods down, the maple in the
oak, the ones that split like stone, is one thing—to
bring them in is block-and-tackle and a long
ride, topped off, sheer and stacked to roll and size on
the double bed of the truck. And the ricochet
of the road doesn't help, at town or mountain
speed, the big load edging one way first, then back.
Most of the time the driver's half dead-drunk,
happy with the weight of the dead world behind
him—shifting with power, downshifting, going with
the curve, the circle inside gravity. He
understands that lumber is alive inside
the tree, that it will fly back up the mountain
in time, fly true, and at a wonderful speed.

10

What we were after was too high for a man
to reach alone, so I stood on his shoulders
and still had to climb—something left behind, some-
thing wished for, something killed. We'd already cut
the thorn and undergrowth and failed hickory trees,
this clearing with its canopy and byplay
of leaves and openness that if you stayed too
long began to bother you, as if the star-
net of sunlight had divided into nerves.
I can't remember what we were after, but
when we went there late at night, solvent, soaked to
the bone, I'd try to sit with him like a man
who knows something and who's figuring the odds
against the time, the flaws, the empty-always.

11

Sunday afternoon, a wind, leaves on the lawn
so dry they rise as if to paper the trees
again. Someone has gathered all the red ones
he can find—he's going to look at them one by
one. From the road the lawn's baronial, deep
to the Home, all the veterans dressed to order.
My mother's second father has a friend here
who's short of breath and speaks through an instrument.
They met at the Somme. The other war's won as
well, so there are younger men my father's age.
And so I'll understand I'm told they're all like
orphans, even the old ones. It's a show, a
kind of holiday, a speech—in other words
the body is a joy or it is hell—.

12

He climbed, they said, the stone ladder, and you could
see it in his face and feel it in the room—
the cloudy colors of stone, the rinsed-out, some-
thing-almost-yellow of the flowers, new, cold.
He pulled, they said, the stone bell-rope of the bell
in heaven, and you could hear it the way you
sometimes hear rain on the edge of a window—
his still hands folded, holding the bell-rope still.
He looked small, the navy uniform too big,
small, and wounded at the center. He slept so
well, they said, because flesh and bone are nothing,
because he was already gone to the snow
and silver palaces. But I touched him
anyway, empty, boy and body, the dream

13

nothing to believe, nothing like the foreign
war in which fathers were sons again, and real.
The train blew by the house filled with airplane parts
and apparatus of the shell and dead steel—
on the sides of the cars the united states
of america in letters large as the
windows soldiers would lean out of waving us
goodbye or windows, coming back, with small flags.
I was a child but I knew that any man
dying was a poverty and that a train
was both the thing itself and the poor memory
of the bodies brought back thousands of foreign
miles, through time and loved country and the hometowns,
to die again, with family, in hallowed ground.

14

Like an angel uncle, whose snow-white sailor
hat I floated in the bath with one of his
shoes, who'd come back from the Pole but too far
north of the war to die—unlike the angel
soldier-sailor sitting like sculpture at the
far foot of his coffin, wings enfolded, his
dark child's-head distracted . . . Those pictures they'll
have of us, in a bled-out brown and white, will
show us walking on our hands or scaling trees
or sitting on the brother step for the one still
absent, and this, with all our sun-at-the-end-of-
the-street-gone-gold-on-green melancholy, will
be the work of a god whose gift is the moment
lost or past, passed on to children of memory.

Stanley Plumly was born in Barnesville, Ohio, in 1939 and grew up in the lumber and farming regions of Virginia and Ohio. His first collection, *In the Outer Dark*, won the Delmore Schwartz Memorial Award; his third, *Out-of-the-Body Travel*, was nominated for the National Book Critics Circle Award. He has received fellowships from the Guggenheim Foundation, the National Endowment for the Arts, and the Ingram-Merrill Foundation. He has taught at many universities around the country, including the Universities of Iowa, Michigan, and Washington, Ohio University, Princeton, and Columbia. He is presently a member of the Department of English at the University of Maryland.